# What happened to Little Treasure?

"She's wrong," Eric whispered. "I'm sure no one stole her dog. It just ran off."

Cam said, "*Click*," again.

"We're just lucky we're on a boat," Eric went on. "Little Treasure could not have gone very far."

Cam opened her eyes.

She told Eric, "When we first saw her on the boat, she had her dog. Then, after she went to see the fireboat, it was gone. Someone in that crowd stole Little Treasure."

"That's silly," Eric said. "No one would steal a dog."

Cam shook her head and told Eric, "That woman looks rich. I think someone took Little Treasure and plans to send a note. *I have your dog. If you want her back, you'll have to pay a ransom, a lot of money.*"

# The Cam Jansen Adventure Series

DON'T FORGET ABOUT THE YOUNG CAM JANSEN
SERIES FOR YOUNGER READERS!

# CamJansen
# The Barking
# Treasure Mystery

### David A. Adler
Illustrated by Susanna Natti

PUFFIN BOOKS

PUFFIN BOOKS
Published by the Penguin Group
Penguin Young Readers Group, 345 Hudson Street, New York, New York 10014, U.S.A.
Penguin Group (Canada), 10 Alcorn Avenue, Toronto, Ontario, Canada M4V 3B2
(a division of Pearson Penguin Canada Inc.)
Penguin Books Ltd, 80 Strand, London WC2R 0RL, England
Penguin Ireland, 25 St Stephen's Green, Dublin 2, Ireland
(a division of Penguin Books Ltd)
Penguin Group (Australia), 250 Camberwell Road, Camberwell, Victoria 3124, Australia (a
division of Pearson Australia Group Pty Ltd)
Penguin Books India Pvt Ltd, 11 Community Centre, Panchsheel Park,
New Delhi - 110 017, India
Penguin Group (NZ), Cnr Airborne and Rosedale Roads, Albany, Auckland,
New Zealand (a division of Pearson New Zealand Ltd)
Penguin Books (South Africa) (Pty) Ltd, 24 Sturdee Avenue, Rosebank,
Johannesburg 2196, South Africa

Registered Offices: Penguin Books Ltd, 80 Strand, London WC2R 0RL, England

First published in the United States of America by Viking,
a division of Penguin Putnam Books for Young Readers, 1999
Published by Puffin Books, a division of Penguin Young Readers Group, 2001, 2005

1 3 5 7 9 10 8 6 4 2

Text copyright © David A. Adler, 1999
Illustrations copyright © Susanna Natti, 1999
All rights reserved

THE LIBRARY OF CONGRESS HAS CATALOGED THE VIKING EDITION AS FOLLOWS:
Adler, David A.
Cam Jansen and the barking treasure mystery / David A. Adler ; illustrated by Susanna
Natti.
p. cm.— (The Cam Jansen series ; 19)
Summary: When a woman's poodle disappears during a boat ride around the city, Cam
uses her photographic memory to solve the mystery.
ISBN 0-670-88516-9 (hardcover)
[1. Dogs—Fiction. 2. Boats and boating—Fiction. 3. Mysteries and detective stories.]
I. Natti, Susanna, ill. II. Title. III. Series: Adler, David A. Cam Jansen adventure; 19.
PZ7.A2615Caab 1999
[Fic]—dc21
98-52517 CIP AC

Puffin Books ISBN 0-14-240319-9

Printed in the United States of America

RL: 2.2

Best wishes for happy reading
to my good friends
Doni, Josh, Demi, and Davey

# Chapter One

"The frog," Mabel Trent said, and laughed. "Do you remember the frog?"

Mrs. Shelton laughed, too. "Of course I remember it. It jumped out of your desk and scared Miss Donovan."

"Poor Miss Donovan," Mabel Trent said. "She dropped her books and yelled at the frog, 'Get out of my class!'"

Mrs. Shelton laughed.

"And you put cream cheese in Mr. Casper's jar of white paint," she said. "You sure did some crazy things."

Cam Jansen whispered to her friend Eric Shelton, "She must have gotten into lots of trouble in school."

"Mom wouldn't laugh if I did those things," Eric said. "She would punish me."

When Mabel Trent was in sixth grade, her family had moved far away. But she and Eric's mother were still good friends. Now she was

visiting the Sheltons. They were waiting in line for a boat ride around the city.

"Look," Eric said. He pointed to a sign. It listed the sights they would see on the ride and the rules for passengers. "Near the end of the ride, we see a pirate ship that is 200 years old."

"I want to remember this list," Cam said. Then she blinked her eyes and said, "*Click*."

Cam has an amazing photographic memory. It's as if she has a camera in her head, with photographs of whatever she has seen. Cam says *"Click"* whenever she wants to remember something. She says it's the sound her mental camera makes.

Cam's real name is Jennifer. But when people found out about her amazing memory, they called her "The Camera." Soon "The Camera" became just "Cam."

Mrs. Shelton bought four tickets. Then they waited in line to go on the boat.

"You'll love this ride, Little Treasure," the

woman in front of them told the small gray poodle in her arms. Then she told the short, bald man in front of her, "I call her Little Treasure because that's what she is."

The woman was wearing a long red dress and lots of expensive jewelry. She carried a large, red leather bag. Little Treasure's collar was red and had jewels in it.

Cam closed her eyes and said, "*Click.*"

"What are you doing?" Eric asked.

"I'm looking at the picture I have of that sign," Cam whispered, with her eyes still closed. "And rule number six says, 'No animals allowed.'"

Cam opened her eyes and said, "They won't allow Little Treasure on board."

The line moved forward. A man in a sailor uniform was taking tickets.

"I'm sorry," he told the woman in the red dress, "but animals are not allowed."

"This is not an animal," she said. "She's my Little Treasure."

4

"Well, she looks like a dog and dogs are not allowed." Then he said, "Next."

Mrs. Shelton gave him the tickets. Then she, Mabel Trent, Cam, and Eric walked onto the deck of the boat.

There were benches outside, along the rail of the deck. There was a covered area, too, with seats and a snack bar.

The boat was crowded. Most of the seats were taken.

"Please, could you move down," Mabel Trent asked a thin man with a bushy beard. He was sitting on a bench by the rail.

The man moved to his left.

Then Mabel Trent asked a short, bald man sitting on the left to move, too. The man didn't seem to hear Mabel Trent.

"Please," she said loudly. "Could you move down?"

"Oh," the man said. He picked up a shopping bag and moved to his right.

"There," Mabel Trent said. "Now we all

have a place to sit and everyone is happy."

"I was happy before," the man with the bushy beard mumbled.

There was a rumbling. Then the boat moved away from the dock.

"Welcome aboard. I am Nancy, your tour guide."

Mabel Trent looked around. Then she called out, "Where are you, Nancy?"

"There she is," Cam said, and pointed to a large speaker box mounted on a metal pole.

Mabel Trent waved to the speaker box and shouted, "I'm glad to meet you, Nancy. I'm Mabel Trent."

"Please look at the large red-brick building on the port side," Nancy announced. "It was once used as a film studio. The movie *Happy Rider* was made there."

"Oh!" Mabel Trent screamed. "I loved *Happy Rider.*" She hurried to the other side of the boat and shouted, "There it is!"

"Look," Cam whispered to Eric.

"I am looking," he said.

"No, over there," Cam told him. She pointed to the woman in the long red dress. "Where's her Little Treasure?"

# Chapter Two

"Maybe she let a friend take care of Little Treasure," Eric whispered.

Cam said, "I don't think so."

"And now," Nancy announced, "take a deep breath. Do you smell something sweet and chewy? That large gray building on the port side is a bubble gum factory."

Eric took a deep breath. Cam didn't. She just watched the woman in the long red dress.

Cam nudged Eric.

"Look at her," Cam whispered. "She's talking to her leather bag."

They watched the woman put her hand in the bag. Then she leaned forward and seemed to be talking to her hand.

Cam whispered to Eric, "I think Little Treasure is in there."

"Look on the starboard side now," Nancy said. "That's the side facing the open sea. You'll see a fireboat."

"That's over there," Mrs. Shelton said, and

pointed to the other side of the boat.

"That's right, a fireboat," Nancy said. "There are fires even here in the water. Well, not really *in* the water, but on boats. The fireboat has hoses and a large pump on board and searchlights for use at night."

"I want to see this," Eric said.

Eric hurried to the starboard side of the boat. Cam went there, too.

The fireboat was not moving. A fireman was standing in the stern of the boat, holding the end of a hose spraying water. A large crowd had gathered by the rail of the tour boat to watch.

Cam and Eric found two places by the rail, just to the right of the woman in the long red dress.

Cam wanted to look into the woman's red leather bag, but she couldn't. The woman held it on her left shoulder.

People crowded all around Cam, Eric, and the woman in the red dress.

"Hey, I want to see. I want to see," a small boy said. He pushed through the crowd. Cam and Eric squeezed together and made room for him by the rail.

"I'm a visitor," Mabel Trent shouted, "and I have a camera. I want to see, too, and I want to take a picture."

Mrs. Shelton stood in the back of the crowd and watched as her friend pushed her way to the rail.

12

The fireman pointed the end of the hose up. Water sprayed high into the air.

"It's like a fountain," Mabel Trent said. She looked through the viewfinder of her camera and pressed the shutter button.

*Click.*

The fireman slowly turned the hose toward the tour boat.

"Don't spray us!" Nancy called to him. "Don't spray us!"

He didn't. He laughed and turned the hose the other way.

As the tour boat moved past the fireboat, people moved away from the rail. Cam followed the woman in the red dress to the back of the boat. The woman looked at Cam and smiled. Cam smiled, too.

Very few people were sitting there.

The woman sat down. She carefully put her red leather bag on the seat to her left. Cam sat next to the bag. Eric sat next to Cam.

Cam tried again to look into the bag.

The woman moved the bag to the seat on her right, away from Cam.

"And now," Nancy announced, "if you look way out on the starboard side, you might be able to see an oil tanker."

Cam, Eric, and the woman turned and looked behind them.

"I can't see it," Eric complained.

"There it is," Cam said, and pointed. She

hurried to the other side of the woman. "You can see it better from here."

While Eric and the woman looked to the right, Cam looked in the woman's bag.

"Oh, my," Cam said. She was surprised. "Your Little Treasure is not in there!"

The woman winked at Cam and said softly, "Of course not. I wouldn't have my Little Treasure in there. Animals are not allowed."

"No," Cam said. "You don't understand. Little Treasure *really* isn't in there!"

The woman looked in her bag.

She put her hand on her chest and sighed. "My treasure, my Little Treasure is gone!"

# Chapter Three

There were tears in the woman's eyes. She still held her hand to her chest and said, "I love my Little Treasure and she loves me."

Eric looked in the bag. Then he said, "Maybe she jumped out."

The woman took a tissue from her bag. She wiped her eyes. "No," she said softly. "Little Treasure is a good dog. She would never jump out."

"Maybe she was frightened," Cam said. "Boat rides can be scary."

"No," the woman insisted. "She's been on boats before. She loves boat rides."

Then the woman said in a loud, sure voice, "She was stolen. Someone reached into my bag and took her out. Lots of people see my Little Treasure and want her."

"We'll tell Nancy," Eric said. "She'll announce that a dog is missing."

Cam said, "We'll tell the captain."

"No," the woman told them, and shook her head. "We won't tell anyone. I snuck Little Treasure on board and *I'll* find her. I'll just walk around the boat and talk. When she hears my voice, she'll run to me."

"And we'll help you," Eric said. "My friend Cam has a photographic memory. She's good at finding things and solving mysteries."

"Good," the woman said. She got up. "Let's do it!"

She walked to the open area of the boat and talked softly. It seemed that she was talking to herself.

"Here I am, Little Treasure," she said. "It's me, Lila. Here I am, Little Treasure," she said again. "It's me, Lila."

Cam and Eric walked to the open area, too. Then Cam stopped. She closed her eyes and said, "*Click.*"

"She's wrong," Eric whispered. "I'm sure no one stole her dog. It just ran off."

Cam said, "*Click,*" again.

"We're just lucky we're on a boat," Eric went on. "Little Treasure could not have gone very far."

"Let's all wave," Nancy announced, "to the two young women water-skiing past us on the starboard side."

Lots of people waved and the water-skiers waved back. But Cam just stood there, with her eyes still closed.

Cam opened her eyes.

She told Eric, "When we first saw her on the boat, she had her dog. Then, after she

18

went to see the fireboat, it was gone. Someone in that crowd stole Little Treasure."

"That's silly," Eric said. "No one would steal
a dog."

Cam shook her head and told Eric, "That
woman looks rich. I think someone took
Little Treasure and plans to send a note. *I
have your dog. If you want her back, you'll have to
pay a ransom, a lot of money.*"

# Chapter Four

"I saw you," Mabel Trent said, as she and Mrs. Shelton walked toward Cam and Eric. "And you didn't wave."

"Eric and Cam are good children," Mrs. Shelton told her. "Let them do what they want."

"But waving is fun," Mabel Trent said. Then she waved to a woman wearing a large straw hat sitting by the rail.

The woman looked at Mabel Trent, but she didn't wave back.

Mabel Trent waved again, this time with both her hands.

The woman pushed the straw hat up, away from her eyes. She looked at Mabel Trent and shook her head.

"Oh, my goodness," Mabel Trent said very loudly. "Don't you remember me?"

Mabel Trent walked quickly to the woman, reached out, and grabbed her hand. She

shook it and asked, "How are you? How are you?"

The woman looked at Mabel Trent and said slowly, "I'm fine."

"Well, you look terrific," Mabel Trent told her. "You look happy and healthy. You look just great!"

"Do you think so? Do you really think so?" the woman asked.

Mabel Trent nodded.

The woman said, "Thank you." She was smiling now.

"And now," Nancy announced, "look to the port side for a great view of the city's skyline. Those of you with cameras might want to take a picture of it."

"That's me," Mabel Trent said. "I have a camera. Bye-bye," she said to the woman with the straw hat, and went off.

"Does Mabel Trent know that woman?" Eric asked his mother.

Mrs. Shelton said, "Probably not. But that

woman is still smiling. That's what Mabel does. She makes people happy."

Mrs. Shelton told Cam and Eric, "Now stay together and don't lean over the rail." Then she hurried to join her friend.

"That Mabel Trent is fun," Eric said. Then he turned to Cam.

Her eyes were closed.

Eric said, "Now we have to find Little Treasure."

Cam said, "*Click*."

"I'm looking at everyone who was near the woman in the red dress when she was watching the fireboat," Cam told Eric.

Cam said, "*Click*," again.

"There was a thin man with a bushy beard," Cam said with her eyes still closed, "that woman with the straw hat, a woman with long blond hair and long earrings, a short, bald man, and a man wearing an orange baseball cap."

Cam opened her eyes.

"One of those people took Little Treasure," Cam told Eric.

"Well," Eric told Cam, "we just saw the woman with the straw hat, and she didn't have Little Treasure."

"So," Cam said, looking around, "that leaves us with four people who may have taken the dog."

"Look," Eric said. "There's a woman with blond hair standing by the snack bar."

Cam and Eric hurried into the covered area of the boat. A woman with long blond hair was buying a cup of soda.

The woman paid for the drink. She said, "Thank you," and turned around.

"That's not her," Cam whispered. "The woman I saw was wearing earrings."

Cam and Eric went outside. They walked slowly along the deck of the boat.

"Here I am, Little Treasure. It's me, Lila," the woman in the red dress said. She smiled at Cam and Eric. Then she walked on and said again, "Here I am, Little Treasure. It's me, Lila."

Two boys laughed as she walked past.

"They think she's talking to herself," Eric whispered. "They think she's crazy."

Cam told Eric, "And *I* think we better hurry and find her dog. We have to find Little Treasure before the ride ends and people start leaving the boat."

Cam and Eric walked slowly along the starboard side. They looked at all the people sitting on the benches along the rail.

Eric grabbed Cam's arm. "Look at him," he whispered, "the man with the orange baseball cap. His jacket is all puffed out. He could be hiding something in there. He could be hiding Little Treasure!"

# Chapter Five

"He was there," Cam whispered. "He was near the woman in the red dress when she was looking at the fireboat."

The man was wearing a short blue jacket. His legs were crossed and he was sitting next to a young woman. They were holding hands and talking.

"Little Treasure is a small dog," Eric whispered. "There's lots of room for her under that jacket."

Cam and Eric watched the man. He said

something to the young woman and she laughed.

"He looks like someone in love," Eric whispered, "not someone who just stole a dog."

"In about ten minutes," Nancy announced, "we will be passing the *Evil Skull,* a pirate ship that is 200 years old. It will be on the port side."

People hurried to get to the port side of the boat. A thin man with a bushy beard walked by. He was carrying a cloth book bag.

"And look at him," Cam said. "He was near the woman in the red dress, too."

Cam turned and watched the man with the bushy beard. Eric watched the man with the orange baseball cap.

"The *Evil Skull* is being restored," Nancy announced. "When that's done, you'll be able to go on board."

The man in the baseball cap said something to the young woman. He uncrossed his legs. Then they both got up to join the people at the port side. When the man stood, his jacket was no longer puffed out. There was no room under it for Little Treasure.

"He didn't take the dog," Eric whispered to Cam. "And I still don't think the dog was stolen. I think she just ran off."

"Look," Cam said, and pointed to the man with the bushy beard. "I'm going to get close to him. Maybe Little Treasure is in that book bag."

"If you look ahead," Nancy announced,

"you can see the *Evil Skull*. Our captain, Captain Kramer, will go past it very slowly, so you can get a good look at a real pirate ship and take lots of pictures."

Cam and Eric walked toward the man.

"Over here! Over here!" Mabel Trent shouted. She wanted Cam and Eric to stand near her and Mrs. Shelton.

"Pretend you don't hear her," Cam whispered. "We have to get close to that man."

By now, there were lots of people crowded around the man. It was hard to get near him.

"Over here!" Mabel Trent yelled again. "I saved you a spot."

Cam and Eric pretended not to hear her.

The woman in the red dress walked past. She was still saying, "Here I am, Little Treasure. It's me, Lila."

Cam and Eric squeezed between two women who were trying to get close to the rail. They were close to the man with the bushy beard.

Then someone screamed, "Help! Help!"

# Chapter Six

The scream came from the covered area of the boat. Cam, Eric, and a few other people ran there.

"It's dark in there and I heard a growl," a tall man yelled, as he ran from the bathroom.

The door was open. The man ran right into Cam.

"I'm sorry. I'm sorry," he told Cam. "But there's some big animal in there."

Then a small poodle, Little Treasure, walked out of the bathroom.

People laughed.

"That's some *big* animal," someone joked.

"Oh, I feel so embarrassed," the man said.

"That's Little Treasure," Eric said, "and I was right. She wasn't stolen. She was just lost."

Eric held out his hands and said, "Come here, Little Treasure. I'll take you to Lila."

Little Treasure ran to Eric. He picked her up.

Cam looked at Eric and Little Treasure. She closed her eyes and said, "*Click.*"

Eric told Cam, "You don't have to *click* anymore. We have the dog. The mystery is solved. Now we can look at the *Evil Skull.*"

"There you are, my Little Treasure," the woman in the red dress said. She hurried to Eric and took the dog in her arms.

"Oh, how can I thank you?" she asked Eric.

"You should thank me," the tall man said. "I found your dog."

Cam opened her eyes. She looked at Little Treasure. Then she closed her eyes again and said, "*Click.*"

"I love you. Yes, I do," the woman in the red dress said, and kissed Little Treasure's nose.

"There it is," Nancy announced. "The *Evil Skull.*"

"Oh, I have to see this," the tall man said. He started toward the port side rail.

"Me too," Eric said.

"Wait!" Cam told them.

She opened her eyes and said, "There's still a mystery here. We have to solve it soon, before the boat docks."

"There's no mystery," the woman in the red dress said. "I have my Little Treasure."

She kissed the dog's nose again and said, "And I'm not putting you in my bag. You'll stay out with me and enjoy the ride like everyone else."

"You have Little Treasure back," Cam said. "But her collar is gone. That's why someone took her into the bathroom, to steal her collar."

"Pirates!" Nancy announced. "Just imagine! There were once pirates on that boat."

"Pirates! Thieves!" Lila said. "There's one on *this* boat. There are diamonds and emeralds in the collar."

# Chapter Seven

"It's a small collar," Lila said. "Someone could put it in a pocket and walk off the boat with it."

Cam looked back at the bathroom door. There was a Men's sign on it.

"Little Treasure was taken into a men's bathroom," Cam said, "so we know it was a man who stole the collar."

"And I know where he is," Eric said. "He's over there, looking at the *Evil Skull*. Everyone is."

Cam closed her eyes and said, "*Click*."

"He's either a thin man with a bushy beard," Cam said with her eyes still closed, "or a short, bald man."

Cam opened her eyes and told the woman in the red dress, "I saw them standing near you when you were looking at the fireboat. That's when Little Treasure was taken."

Cam, Eric, and Lila went to the port side. People were crowded against the rail, looking at the *Evil Skull*. But Cam, Eric, and Lila saw only their backs.

"I see two tall, thin men," Eric said. He pointed to both of them. "But from here, I can't tell if they have bushy beards."

"And I don't see any short, bald men," Lila said. "It's hard to find short people in a crowd."

"We have to get to the rail," Cam told them. "Then we can turn around and look at everyone."

Lila tapped a woman and said, "Excuse me, I have to get to the front."

The woman told Lila, "I'm sorry, but I want to see, too."

Cam and Eric got behind one of the thin men. They tried to see if he had a beard.

"I have an idea," Eric whispered. Then he said loudly, "I'm just a child. I can't see anything from here."

"Oh, of course," the man said. "Let the boy through."

He turned and made room for Cam and Eric. Cam looked up. The man had no beard.

A woman and another man made room for Cam and Eric. Soon they were in the middle of the crowd. They looked for the man with the bushy beard and the short, bald man.

"There you are," Mabel Trent said loudly. "I've saved a place for you."

Cam and Eric moved next to Mrs. Shelton and Mabel Trent. Then they turned and faced the crowd.

"There he is," Eric said. "There's the man with the bushy beard!"

"There's who?" Mrs. Shelton asked.

Mabel Trent said, "You're both looking the wrong way. The *Evil Skull* isn't over there. It's this way! It's in the water!"

Cam opened her eyes and said, "Yes, that's him. Let's get Lila."

# Chapter Eight

Cam and Eric hurried through the crowd. They found Lila in the back of the boat. That was where everyone would get off when the boat docked. A short, bald man carrying a shopping bag was there, too.

*Ruff! Ruff!*

"Don't worry," Lila told Little Treasure. "He won't take you away from me."

Then she asked Cam, "Was he standing near me when Little Treasure was taken?"

"I'll bet he was," Eric said. "And I bet he took Little Treasure. Everyone else is looking at the pirate ship. But he's here. He wanted to be the first one off when the boat docked."

"I don't know what you're talking about," the man said.

Cam closed her eyes and said, "*Click*." She looked at the picture she had in her head of the people who were standing near Lila before. Then she opened her eyes and looked at the man.

"Yes," Cam said. "He and the thin man with the bushy beard were next to you when you looked at the fireboat."

"So what?" the man asked. "I can stand next to anyone I want!"

The man looked around. The boat was still a long way from land. There was no place he could go.

Cam closed her eyes again and said, "*Click*."

"He's the same man who was standing in front of you before we boarded the boat," Cam said, with her eyes still closed. "He saw the jewels in Little Treasure's collar."

"Nancy! Nancy!" Lila called.

An old, short woman with long white hair, wearing a long bead necklace, came from the covered area. "I'm Nancy," she said.

Then she looked at Little Treasure and told Lila, "We don't allow dogs on this boat."

Lila pointed to the man and said, "But he stole my dog's collar."

"That's silly," the man said. "What would I do with a dog's collar?"

"There are jewels on it," Eric said.

"Go up the ladder to the right of the snack bar," Nancy said to Cam and Eric. "Tell Captain Kramer I need him."

Cam and Eric hurried to the covered area of the boat. As they climbed the ladder Cam called, "Captain Kramer! Captain Kramer!"

Two men, one young and one old, were sitting in the small cabin. They both turned. In front of them was a large wheel and lots of dials.

The old man said, "I'm Captain Kramer."

"There's a man and a dog and jewels," Eric said really fast. "It's a collar, Little Treasure's, and he has it."

The two men looked at each other. They didn't know what Eric was telling them.

Then Cam said slowly, "Nancy said she needs you."

"Take the wheel, Josh," Captain Kramer

told the young man. Then he followed Cam and Eric.

"He stole my dog's collar," Lila said, and pointed to the short, bald man. "There are jewels on it."

The man said, "You should tell her that dogs are not allowed."

Captain Kramer stepped toward the man.

"I don't even have a dog," the man said. "What would I do with a collar?"

Captain Kramer took another step toward the man.

"I didn't know it had diamonds and emeralds," the man said.

"She said it had *jewels*!" Cam said, pointing to the woman in the red dress. "That man knows what jewels they are because he stole them!"

# Chapter Nine

"May I look in your bag?" Captain Kramer asked.

The man smiled and said, "Sure."

He gave Captain Kramer the shopping bag. Captain Kramer reached into the bag and took out two books.

"Look at this," Cam said. She found a few short hairs on the books. "Gray hairs, just like Little Treasure's."

Captain Kramer said, "Please empty your pockets."

The man looked over the edge of the boat.

They were still far from the dock. Then he slowly reached into his pocket and took out the collar and gave it to Captain Kramer. The captain gave it to Lila.

*Ruff! Ruff!*

"Don't you go anywhere," Captain Kramer told the man.

People started to gather, to be ready to get off when the boat docked.

"There you are," Mrs. Shelton said to Cam and Eric.

"You missed the best part of the ride," Mabel Trent told them.

"No, they didn't," Lila said. "They caught a real pirate." She pointed to the thief and said, "He stole Little Treasure's collar."

Then Lila took some money from her pocket and gave it to Eric.

"No, thank you," Eric said. "We don't need to be paid."

"I just want to thank you," Lila said. "And I want each of you to buy something, a book or a toy."

Cam and Eric said, "Thank you."

Just then the boat moved close to the dock. The man in the sailor uniform was standing there, ready to help people get off the boat. The thief jumped onto the dock and started to run.

"Get him!" Captain Kramer yelled. "Call the police!"

The man in the sailor uniform grabbed and held the thief. Then he blew a whistle. Two police officers came quickly.

Then the boat docked and people started to get off.

"Please," Captain Kramer said to Cam, Eric, Nancy, and the others, "stay here for a few minutes."

They watched Captain Kramer talk to the police. One of the police officers asked Lila to join them. They spoke some more. Then the police put handcuffs on the thief and took him away. Lila went with them.

Captain Kramer came back on the boat. He said to Cam and Eric, "Lila told us how you helped catch the thief."

He took four tickets from his pocket and gave them to Cam. "You were too busy to see a lot of the sights," he said, "so I'd like you to come back, as my guests."

Cam, Eric, and Mrs. Shelton said, "Thank you."

Mabel Trent said, "I'm going home tomorrow."

"You can go on our next tour. It starts in one hour," Nancy said.

"Can we go again?" Mabel Trent asked Mrs. Shelton.

Mrs. Shelton looked at Cam and Eric. Then she smiled and said, "Sure, we can go again."

"Good," Mabel Trent said. She put her arm over Nancy's shoulder and told her, "You are *so* lucky! I'll help you give the next tour. I'll tell people about the sights and I'll tell jokes. And I don't even need the speaker box. I can talk *really* loud."

"She sure can," Mrs. Shelton said, and laughed.

Cam and Eric laughed, too, and so did Mabel Trent.

Cam Jansen has a great memory. Do you?
Look at the picture on page 53.
Blink your eyes, say, "*Click!*"
and then turn back to this page.
How much do you remember?

1. How many people are on the boat?
2. Is anyone wearing eyeglasses?
3. Is Mrs. Wood on or off the boat?
4. Who is carrying the thief's shopping bag?
5. Who is holding the tickets?
6. Can you describe Captain Kramer?
   Is he wearing a jacket? A necktie?
   Does he have a beard? A mustache?
   Is he smiling at Cam?

Play memory games with a friend.
Study other pictures in
*Cam Jansen and the Barking Treasure Mystery*
and ask each other questions.